Angelina's Dance of Friendship

Angelina Ballerina™

Published by Pleasant Company Publications
© 2004 Helen Craig Limited and Katharine Holabird
Based on the text by Katharine Holabird and the illustrations by Helen Craig
From the script by James Mason

Visit our Web site at www.americangirl.com and
Angelina's very own site at www.angelinaballerina.com.

Printed in the United States of America.

04 05 06 07 08 09 10 NGS 10 9 8 7 6 5 4 3 2

Angelina's Dance of Friendship

PLEASANT COMPANY PUBLICATIONS

"Well done, my darlings!" exclaimed Miss Lilly at the end of ballet class. "Now, before you go, I have some news."

The mouselings gathered around Miss Lilly.

"I am sure you remember Anya Moussorsky, who visited us from Dacovia last year," said Miss Lilly. "Anya is coming to Chipping Cheddar this summer to learn ballet."

"Oh, Alice!" Angelina squealed as she grabbed her best friend's paws and spun her in a circle. "Isn't that wonderful?"

That evening, Angelina pleaded with her mother to let
Anya stay at their house for the summer. "Please, Mum,"
said Angelina. "She won't be any trouble!"

"Of course she won't," said Mrs. Mouseling. "But where
will she sleep?"

"In my room," Angelina chattered. "Dad will move another bed in, won't you, Dad?" She tugged her father's arm gently.

Mr. Mouseling set down his newspaper. "It'll be a tight squeeze…" he said thoughtfully.

"And it's for a long time," added Mrs. Mouseling.

But Angelina was determined. "I don't mind," she insisted. "I *want* to share my room!"

Angelina's room *was* a bit crowded with two beds, but
Angelina was too excited to care.

"We're going to have the best summer ever," she said
when Anya finally arrived. "We'll share everything!"

Angelina tucked Anya's books beside her own on the windowsill. She cleared some space on the nightstand for Anya's picture of her parents. And she pulled a pink tutu out of her closet for Anya to wear to ballet class.

"Thanks, Angelina," said Anya, "but I've never done ballet before. What if I don't fit in?"

Angelina put an arm around her new friend. "Don't worry, Anya," she said. "I'll look after you. I promise."

At ballet class the next day, Anya worked very hard to follow Angelina's steps.

"You dance so well, Anya!" exclaimed Alice when the music ended. "It's as if you've been doing ballet for ages."

When Miss Lilly asked the mouselings to choose partners to make up a special dance, Angelina was worried. Would Alice be hurt if Angelina danced with Anya? But Alice didn't mind at all, and Anya had a wonderful idea—she and Angelina would dance the story of the kingfishers.

"It's a Dacovian story," explained Anya, "about two kingfishers who are good friends and stay together their whole lives."

"How lovely!" said Miss Lilly. "A dance of friendship." She pulled the two mouselings into a warm embrace.

Angelina and Anya practiced their special dance every day at ballet class. Anya's steps had become as graceful as Angelina's.

"Anya, you are doing so well!" Miss Lilly said when the partners finished their dance.

Then Miss Lilly pulled Angelina aside. "The Dacovian Ballet is coming to the Theatre Royal again," said Miss Lilly. "I think it's a good idea for me to invite Anya this year, don't you?"

Angelina was terribly disappointed. Miss Lilly always took *her* to the Dacovian Ballet. It wasn't fair!

But "Yes, Miss Lilly" was all Angelina could say.

"Good, then," said Miss Lilly, patting Angelina's shoulder. "And tell your mother I'm looking forward to dinner tonight."

That evening, everyone fussed over the Dacovian dinner that Anya had helped to prepare.

"I'm going to show Mrs. Mouseling how to make cheese soufflé, too," Anya said to Miss Lilly, who sat across the table from her.

Angelina sighed and played with her food. She wished she could think of something else to talk about. Then she spotted the kingfisher costumes hanging in the corner. "What do you think of our costumes, Miss Lilly?" Angelina asked brightly.

"They're beautiful!" said Miss Lilly. "Anya is learning ballet so fast," she said to Mrs. Mouseling. "Soon she'll apply to the Dacovian Ballet Academy!"

Anya, Anya, Anya, thought Angelina miserably. Why wouldn't everyone stop talking about Anya?

After dinner, Angelina found Anya sitting in the dark bedroom, staring at the picture of her parents. She looked lonely, and for a moment, Angelina felt sorry for her. Then Angelina realized *where* Anya was sitting.

"That's my bed!" Angelina snapped.

Anya jumped off the bed in surprise. "Oh!" she said. "But I thought we were sharing everything."

"I'm not so sure now," said Angelina. Jealous, angry words tumbled out of her mouth. "I'm tired of hearing about how talented you are," Angelina cried. "And how great Dacovia is. Maybe you just should have stayed there!"

When Angelina awoke the next morning, she was feeling very sorry for the way she had acted. But when she turned to apologize to Anya, Angelina saw that Anya's bed was empty.

Angelina raced downstairs to the kitchen. "Have you seen Anya?" Angelina asked her mother desperately.

"No," said Mrs. Mouseling. "Isn't she in your room?"

Angelina rushed out the front door without answering, but the sound of the ringing telephone called her back.

"Oh, hello, Miss Lilly," said Mrs. Mouseling into the receiver. "Anya's at your house? Good gracious! I had no idea!"

Angelina sat, her head hung low, in Miss Lilly's parlor. She was too ashamed to look at Miss Lilly.

"I'm very disappointed in you," said Miss Lilly. "How would you like to be away from your parents for such a long time?"

"I wouldn't," Angelina answered in a small voice. "Oh, I've been so horrid to Anya! Please may I see her and apologize?"

"Of course you may," said Miss Lilly. She disappeared down the hall, and Angelina waited nervously in the parlor.

But when Miss Lilly returned, Anya wasn't with her. "I'm sorry," said Miss Lilly gently, "but Anya doesn't wish to see you. Perhaps you can speak to her at ballet class."

Angelina's heart sank. Would Anya ever forgive her?

At ballet class, Angelina spotted Anya across the room, talking with William. Angelina took a deep breath, then hurried over.

But Anya wasn't happy to see Angelina. "I don't want to dance with you," Anya said frostily. "I'm dancing with Alice."

After class, a very sad Angelina trudged home beside Alice. "I just wish she'd let me apologize," said Angelina.

Alice felt terrible. "I wish I could help," she said. "Anya wants to practice with me down by the river, wearing your costumes so that we'll feel like real kingfishers."

Angelina stopped in her tracks and smiled thoughtfully. Now she knew *just* how to apologize to Anya.

Angelina dressed in her kingfisher costume and hurried
down to the river. Anya was already there. "Hi, Alice!"
Anya called.

Angelina breathed a sigh of relief as she took her starting
position. Anya didn't recognize her!

On the count of three, the mouselings began to dance across the grassy riverbank. They fluttered apart and then swooped back together, just like real kingfishers. They dipped low and rose up again, wings outstretched.

When the dance ended, Angelina pulled off her mask. "I'm sorry, Anya," she whispered anxiously, hoping Anya wouldn't be angry that she had been fooled.

Anya was silent for a moment, and then she burst into tears. "I'm sorry, too!" she cried. She threw her arms open wide, and the two friends hugged each other tightly.

Angelina and Anya sat together in a bus seat, chattering excitedly. "Wasn't the prince amazing?" said Angelina.

"Oh, yes," said Anya. "Thank you, Miss Lilly. It was the best show I've ever seen!"

Miss Lilly, who was seated behind the two mouselings, leaned forward. "And to think," she said, "that my darling Angelina believed she wasn't going to the Dacovian Ballet this year, when I had three tickets all along!"

That evening, Anya started packing her things, for tomorrow she would return home. She handed the pink tutu to Angelina.

"Oh, no," Angelina insisted. "Keep it. What's mine is yours, remember?" she said warmly, and *this* time, Angelina truly meant it.